The Sunflower Soul

Devpriya Dang

The Sunflower Soul
by
Devpriya Dang©
[Ludhiana, Punjab, India]

ISBN: 978-93-343-5336-5
2025

Cover artwork by Dikshita Saikia
Illustrations by Devpriya Dang

DEDICATION

This book is dedicated to the person who is my home.

CONTENTS

BEING IN LOVE

A place named love
A place
Where, when you hold hands,
You set each other free.
A place
Where, when you nurture and water each other,
You bloom independently.
Flowers,
Varying In colours,
With bold hues and idiosyncrasies,
Yet strikingly beautiful while existing together.
A place
Where you climb singly,
Yet walk alongside, moving in parallel.
A place
Where one talks,
The other understands.
A place
Where one listens,
The other feels heard.
A place
Where "together" you can have your alone solitude
And yet, not feel lonely.
Have you ever been to such a place?
A place named love.

It's beautiful
How someone's happiness can mean so much to a human heart,
Every time your beloved looks dejected,
You're ready to upend the world,
To adorn their lips with a hearty smile.
You do more than you ever believed you could do for someone.
You do it unconsciously.
You do it unapologetically.
You do it, without even trying.
You go a bit further,
Pulling out all the stops,
Moving heaven and earth–
Just for a smile.
A smile that means the world to you.
A world you wish to keep illuminated, always.

He built a huge wall around himself, brick by brick.
Every brick he placed was born from the deceit he suffered in love.

Some saw the wall and walked away,
Assuming it to be an abandoned place.

Some stood by the wall,
But couldn't bear the midnight screams,
Echoing from the other side.
They ran,
Believing it to be a cursed, demonic place.

Some peered through the cracks,
But walked away laughing,
Seeing only barren land.

But here I stand,
Trying to reach the other side unseen.
I long to water the tender seeds lying beneath the soil–
The ones they couldn't see.

For my heart knows the reason behind those night wails.
Oh, honey, your heart is my favorite haunt,
A place where I wish to anchor my soul forever.

"*Never look a gift horse in the mouth*", they say,
And time is one such gift–
The most valuable spell,
A precious emblem to offer
To those you treasure most.

The time you invest and devote
Is a piece of your life you freely give.
And if that's not special,
I don't know what is.

When you like someone,
You want them.

When you love someone,
You already have them.
You have them in your thoughts,
In your prayers,
In your actions.

Desire fades,
And only love pervades.

I wish I could show you,
How much of me longs for so much of you.
I wish I could show you.

My human reflection,
The more I observe new dimensions of love,
The more I witness many ways love is expressed,
The more your way of loving becomes my favorite.
The more your unique expression of love becomes the only one I wish to witness,
For just when I contemplated and asked myself, "Who am I"?
The next moment, I found myself seeing "You in Me".

You will know when you see your world in their eyes,
You will know when, glancing at them, their smile
Lights up your own eyes.

You will know when they become your favorite cartoon character,
And you let out a loud guffaw
As they smirk and play with their face.

All you'll intensely feel is your soul connecting with theirs.
You will know when all you wish for is their fortune and happiness.
Happiness, their lips have yet to find.
Happiness, that could make them ecstatic.
Happiness, their heart will forever hold.

You will know when your brain
loses control over your limbs,
And your eyes search for them,
Your hands crave their touch,
And your feet?
They'll run marathons to catch a glimpse.

You will know it then.

The enticing scent of petrichor inspired this:
No matter where you are,
Have you ever felt that deeply etched craving?
When it rains,
You long to run out there,
With the one you love.

As your hands calmly intertwine,
Braiding loosely with one another.
You gain not just sustenance,
But a sense of emotional security.

As the rain drizzles in the background,
You let it touch the untouched feelings.
Guiding your steps as you dance together,
Adding giggles, smiles, and shyness.
Letting it drench your soul,
And you two,
Fall into a trance together.

You are Earth to my moon–
Distant,
Yet connected to my barren land,
Revolving around your blue–green world.

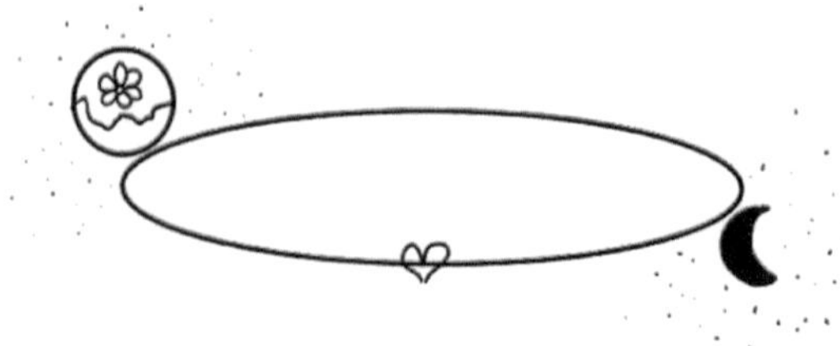

She wished for an incessant night,
With no crack of dawn.
If she could hold onto this moment,
She would keep it forever long.

Securely,
Intimately,
Holding it intact.

The moment of being one,
Wrapped in the silence of eternity.

A Talk Under The Stars

The way you instill love,
Without touching,
Without intending,
Without trying,
Could make angels smile coyly.

She wished a love, that felt like the wide sky!
Colossal and unending.
Where she could fly high,
Without being afraid to fall.
Where brisk hues,
Played their melody.
A sky,
Where winds guided her way back home.
Where birds flocked their wings,
And chirped symphonies of abundance in her ears.
Where the sun brightened her darkest paths
Healing her wounds.
And the moon brought her an enhanced sense of peace.
She wished a love, that felt like the wide sky.

HEARTBREAK

It's strange,
How the person who once made you believe in love
Is the same one who caused you to lose faith in its very existence.
It's strange,
How the love you once practiced like a holy ritual
Has now made you feel as if you've been stung by a curse.
I knew you were nothing less than magic–
Black Magic.

I mean,
Isn't love meant to bring ease to life,
Rather than lead you into a harder one?
Isn't love meant to hold you close,
And warm you on your darkest, coldest days,
Rather than cast you out,
Subjugating you to darkness,
Siphoning the life from you,
And leaving you numb inside?

Isn't love about simplicity, not complexity?
Isn't love about peace,
And not chaos?

Truth
Is like sand in the hand.
The harder you try to hold it,
The harder it slips away.
With every forceful clench of the fist,
The sand escapes.

And just like that,
Your truth spilled.
I tried hard to gather it,
Grain by grain,
Just so I could hide it from others,
Just so I could hide it from myself,
Pretending it didn't exist.
But your ugly truth left my hands dirty.

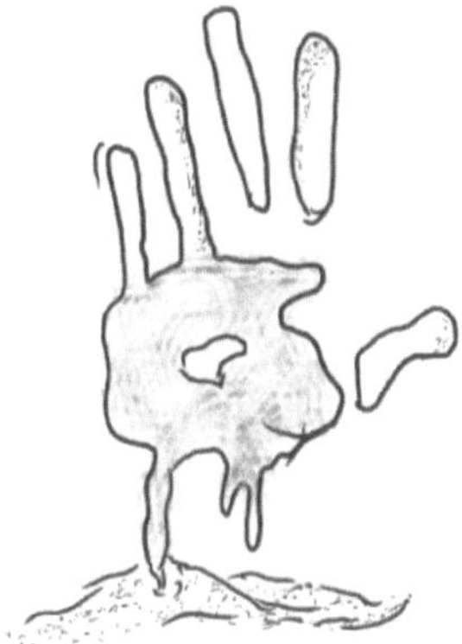

The most ironically dangerous thing about deceiving yourself is that,
You use your brain to fool your brain.

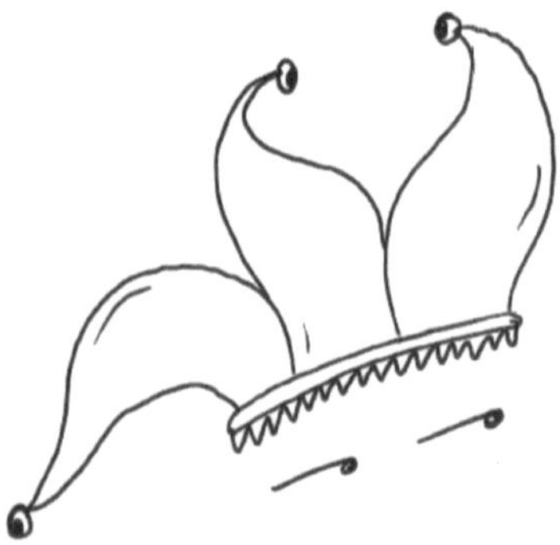

He treated my brain akin to the walls of a rehabilitation center–
Thrashing down the windowpanes,
Pelting them with his harsh words,
Scribbling the walls with his insecurities
And horrifying portraits of narcissistic beliefs.
He drilled a hole,
Hammered it with nails of lie and deceit,
So he could hang my innocence on one such nail,
And desperately stare at it,
His eyes bloodshot with unfulfilled desires.

He treated my mind like the walls of a rehabilitation center,
And when he left,
He left me emotionally drained,
With malignant scabs of anxiety protruding here and there,
With all his baneful scars and marks on me.
And when he left,
He left me devastated.

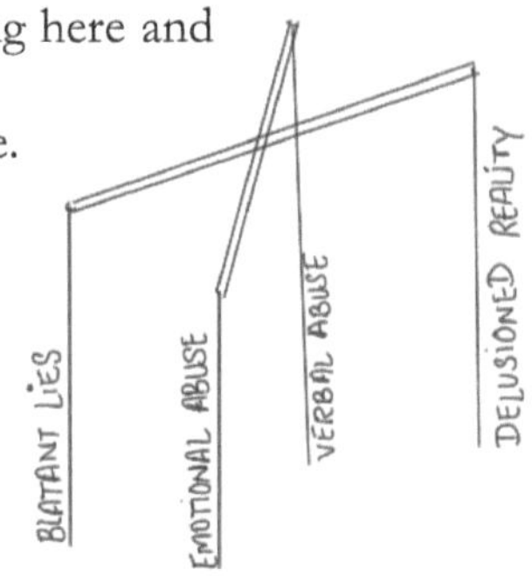

It's funny!
Their protagonism, like a thorny rose,
Rubbing against the same skin.
Tragically funny!

You soothe me before you loot me,
Whispering about thorns and petals.

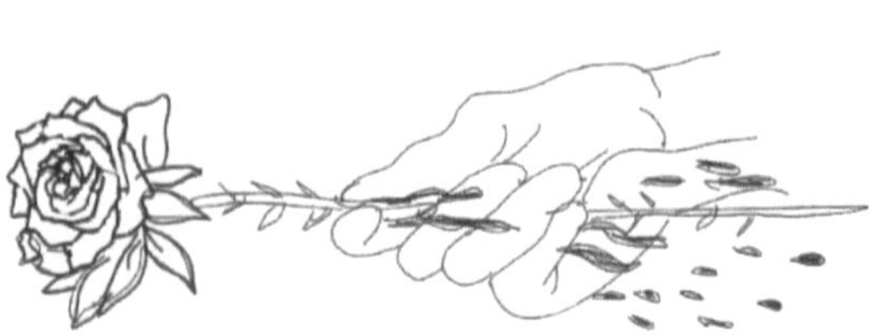

I didn't just miss you on my rough days or the gloomy ones.
I could bear them all alone–
All the pain,
All the sorrow.
All of it.

Rather, the days I missed you the most
Were the joyous ones.
I wondered,
How could your presence have added to the happiness?
What I couldn't bear in those moments
Was the weight of the happiness my lips carried.

"Happiness," you were not a reason for.
"Happiness," you weren't there to cherish.
"Happiness" in those moments when you were not around.
On those days when the world saw me smile,
What they couldn't see was the guilt accompanying it.

I was never found guilty.

My dear,
Please don't rush!
Don't rush after people who committed to stay,
Because if they truly wanted to be with you,
You wouldn't find yourself running,
Turning breathless, stumbling, and getting bruised.

Know, that your affectionate heart
Won't ever let you come to a halt,
So wait, stop, and observe.
Observe the pattern that's unfolding.
Observe how your feelings fluctuate
In response to their misleading actions.
Observe the loop you've dragged yourself into.
Observe and witness how you've been fooling yourself all this time.

Accept it and be bold.
Be brave enough to witness the truth.
Refuse to take another step
Towards someone not ready to walk alongside you.

Cut the chords.

From centuries,
Countless books have been inked,
In search of the answer
To this one rhetorical question:
How do you stop loving someone?
When you have to,
But you don't wish to.

But do we really need to?

You fear losing the people you love.
On the contrary, I am petrified
Of letting in those who claim to love me.
Afraid of the storm they might bring,
Blowing away my flame, struggling to survive.
Afraid of the deep damage they could cause.
Afraid of the old, cracked crevices they might touch,
Not with an intention of healing,
But scraping and speculating.
I am terrified already.

I fear
Losing the whole of me
On the journey to find my other half.
I fear
Self–deprecation,
While
Seeking reverence from another.
And these fears
Make up the bricks of my wall.

An Emotional Tension Between Desire And Fear
You see, we run after human cravings,
And when we quench them,
We begin to run away.
That's how fickle–minded we are.
We pour everything in, only to get back nothing.
And when good unexpectedly comes our way,
We find it clogging our personal space,
And we run, again.
We run hard,
Trying to keep ourselves free from all human interventions and attachments.
We turn breathless,
Gasping for air,
Choking on it altogether.

You scarred my body,
But you could never defile my soul.

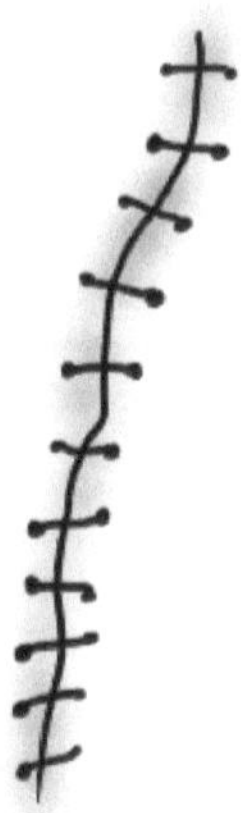

Unlearning Love

When you were vulnerable,
Utterly vulnerable,
When you trampled your heart
And spilled it out completely,
Without caring about the consequences,
Without fear or doubt,
You were met with
Coldness,
Hatred,
And deceit.

How could you unlearn
What this ordeal taught you,
To open up your heart
And love someone again?
How could you shed the dust
That storms left behind,
Which have coagulated on the guards you built
To protect yourself?

What empaths are left with,
After giving more than they get,
Is an internal wrestle,
A deep turmoil.
Something so personal,
So close,
A projection of somebody else's "lows".
It begins to linger,
As if it's there to stay.
They are pretending to be themselves,
But the turmoil,
It keeps getting in the way.

I was pouring out
What I had deep inside.
I poured out so much
Quenching the last few drops,
Leaving nothing behind for myself.
Now, having drained myself,
I still couldn't stop being a one–sided giver.
I began to shred myself,
Bit by bit,
Inch by inch,
For my giving knew no boundaries,
And neither did their receiving.

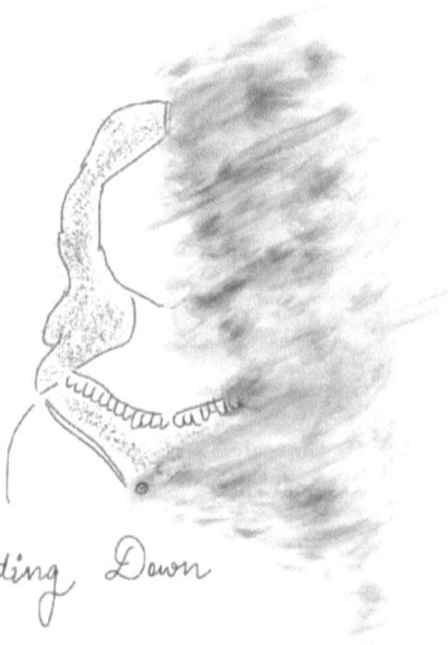

Shredding Down

As an empathic giver,
You start to run.
Running with the leftover love inside you,
So nobody knows.
After all this "being in love",
And after all this giving,
You're still left with a few drops in your vacuous pitcher,
Drops that could fill someone's ocean again.

But you're too scared, to acknowledge it–
That you're not empty,
That you could love again,
And this time,
You could direct it back to yourself.

Yet you don't whisper this to your consciousness,
Because you know you are an unconscious giver,
And you might drain what's left,
Quenching someone's thirst, again–
Someone, who would walk over you,
After using you.

So, you choose to fool others, and yourself,
Into believing
That you are incapable
Of loving,
Or being loved, ever.

Let it touch the untouched spots in your heart,
And allow it to send shivers through your soul.
Let it run down your veins,
Pouring from the open wounds of your fingertips.
Let it coagulate in certain places,
Let it run off in others.

Allow the pain to escape from your eyes,
And stumble from your mouth as you stammer.
Set no barrier.
Let this pain make you feel too much,
Let it burn you down to ashes,
And help the phoenix rise again.
Allow the pain to make you feel alive.

A transformative and cathartic journey.

join the dots

Between Thought And Belief

11:11
Is this how it's supposed to be?
Or was there never anything to suppose or presume?
Was destiny a myth?
And was my inner calling simply a wrong–dialed number?

My belief refuses to follow this path.
It refuses to die a suicidal death
Of my mind's self–destructive thoughts,
Of my body's self–destructive actions.

BEING OUT OF LOVE

EMOTIONAL SURFACING OF TRAUMA

So Much, Yet Nothing

Trigger warning

Sometimes, you feel "so much" of "absolutely nothing".
Like a darted jar, brimming with emptiness.

Existential Crises– Surviving The Self

Will I survive
And get past this, without being defiled?
Will my intent remain aligned with "what it is",
Or will it dilute to what the world deems
"How it should be"?

Drowning In Proportions

Swimming through the gusty storm,
And surviving some mind–numbing tides,
Has ushered me to a place,
Where everything within me has turned to half its proportion.
Half drowned,
Half choked,
Half–hearted,
And
Half soaked.

The Vault Of Secrets

We all have that little corner inside our heads,
A vast, hidden space,
Where lies are denied entry,
Here, we've carved a dark tunnel of truths–
Truths we're too ashamed to confront,
Too afraid to face,
Too skilled at hiding,
Too shy to confess,
Too pained to acknowledge and feel.

Bitter, harsh, shaded truths,
All dumped in the dark.

Between Dismay And Dreams

There's a space inside your heart,
Blank and void.
When your brain connects to it,
Someday, needlessly,
It reflects–
A mirror image of emptiness.

You feel nothing.
Absolutely nothing but emptiness.
Your mind strikes a gloomy chord,
On others, a peaceful one.
This void can be comforting,
Yet it can also feel like a cage.

Sometimes, you sense no escape,
Running breathlessly in a maze,
Seeking a way out.

This space holds echoes of past dismay,
Shadows of present fears,
And the weight of simply surviving.
But, within it also lies a quiet power–
The power to shape your future.
A haunting place that becomes home.

The Winter Within

There will be days
When you feel exhausted,
Of being the only one radiating warmth.
Warmth that once kept you safe, too.

And then, on a random winter morning,
A cold wave strikes,
Like frost on bare skin,
With a dull, pale moon hanging above,
Sending chills down your spine.

Your inner warmth,
It no longer suffices.
It no longer shields you from the falling winter flakes.
And you begin to crave warmth–
More of it, this time.

Warmth,
That could kindle love within.
Warmth,
That could make you feel safe.
Warmth,
That feels like home.

Because some days,
You yearn to be wrapped in the very warmth
You've given so freely to others.

Seeking Out Help
You believe it makes you strong–
This resistance to seeking help.
But in reality,
It's a cool breeze that turns tragic,
Striking you cold, leaving you excruciated and alone.

The real turmoil ignites within,
A battle between heart and mind,
With opposites pulling you apart.

The heart, weary of solving everything alone,
Yearns for a savior,
Longs to be held, understood.

Yet, the mind–
Rigid, robotic, conditioned by hyper–independence,
Refuses to bend.

And in that tension,
Unresolved traumas rise to the surface,
Manifesting in your body,
Seeking release.

Those I Worry For
I never worried for the ones who voiced their feelings–
Who could write, post, or openly express.
I worried for the silent ones.

The ones who bottled up their emotions,
Locking their hearts tight,
Suppressing every urge to release their pain,
Fearing judgment, distrust, and rejection.

I worried for those
Who suffer silently under the weight of perception,
Who hesitate before every step,
Imagining the consequences of being vulnerable.

Those who adhere to their fears,
Convincing themselves it's the truth,
Their reality,
Their destiny.
I worry for those
Who think suffering in silence is safer
Than seeking help.

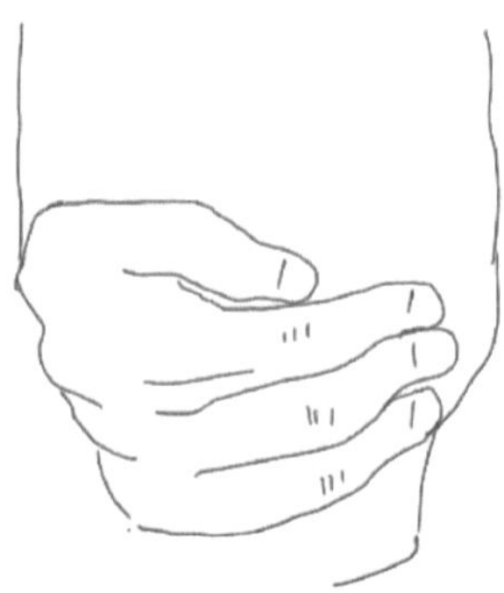

PHYSICAL SURFACING OF TRAUMA

Self–Inflicted Shadows

It's treacherous–
The way we react when pain takes hold.
How we invite more of it,
Letting it seep deeper,
Craving the sting as it lingers.

We become punching bags,
Testing our limits,
Seeing how far we can dive into the darkness
And still resurface.

We wonder how much we can endure–
How many hits we can take
Before we break.

We slip into self–oblivion,
Turning against ourselves,
Engulfed in waves of self–loathing
Beyond our control,
Until someone–
Or something–
Finally turns it off for us.

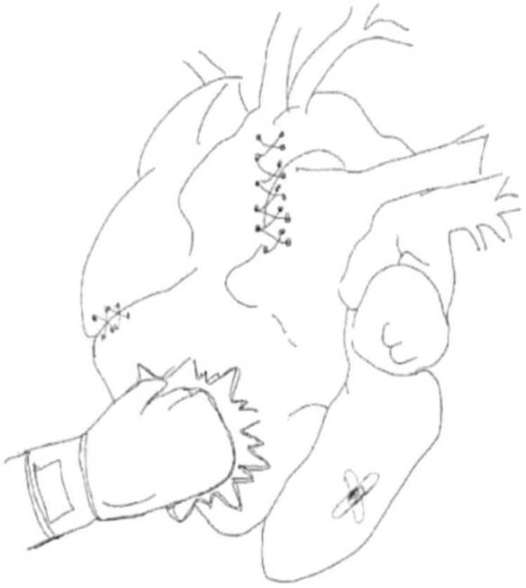

The Shape Of Anxiety
What does anxiety look like?
It begins as a whisper–
A rush of tangled emotions.
Tearless days,
Followed by torrents that won't stop.

The heart races;
The mind numbs.
Roots dig deep,
Spreading with every tick of the clock,
Clenching intellect,
Feeding thoughts of self–loathing and destruction.

In the mirror's gaze,
A hand rises,
Tracing scars on forgotten flesh,
Each touch a silent scream,
Each mark a memory unembraced.

Time marches on;
And anxiety tightens its grip.
Now it flows within–
In the bloodstream, beneath the skin,
An unwelcomed companion,
A way of life.

Hopelessly Romantic

You know,
How traumatizing it feels–
Killing your expectations,
Not by growing immune to affection,
But by faking disdain for it.

And this time,
The world watched me pretend,
Armor on, shields up,
Hiding behind the easiest lie.
Pretending was a refuge;
Lowering my expectations,
The hardest thing to practice.

So, I chose to dislike love,
Or the gestures that convey it.
As I was delusional into believing
I convinced myself–
Love lived in words, not actions.
A fleeting thought, not a lasting state.
Something owned to others, never to oneself.

That's how you turn" hopelessly romantic"–
To the world,
And maybe to yourself too.

I felt numb inside,
Paralyzed, too.
Pretending had now become an exhausting act,
Yet, the depths of pain, hurt, guilt, and fear
I carried within
Seemed boundless,
Like an ocean with no shore.

My eyes are weary, steeped in shadows,
Burdened by the darkness they've embraced.
Exhausted from waiting for a light,
This darkness is too sharp–
With no path for the light of hope to pierce.

Now, my vision falters,
A fog drapes my weary mind.
My senses, dulled and disenchanted,
Refuse to seek or savor simple pleasures.

I am an empty vessel,
Too tired to feel,
Too drained to recall the gentle warmth of light.

Manifestation Of Trauma– A Suicide Attempt In Mind
It's too much,
And you've had enough.
You've admitted that this pain will die with you–
Maybe it should have been given time,
But you want it to end now.

The resentment, the shame, the guilt,
The threats you've carried so long–
They'll die with your death,
So, you choose this over enduring more.
You choose an end,
Because the weight is too much to carry any longer.

Death Bed

What if I told them,
That they would no longer see me?
They would never hear from me again,
As I will be long gone–
Will they still act mean?

The ones who belittled me behind my back–
Would they still choose to do that?
Would they still meet me
With their wall of ego between us?
Would they hold grudges in their hearts,
Forgetting all the good I did?

Will they still serve me with a lie,
When it's the last time they see me?
What if they knew that it was our final moment?
Would they come over,
And ask how I truly felt?
What made me happy?
What sins did I bury inside
That drove me to madness?
Would they sit with me and listen,
Without judgments, without hidden motives,
Without any demands?
Would they be kind?
Generous, Sensitive, loyal?
Would they love me?

Sometimes,
The world feels like an icky place to be.
It makes you guilty
For sins, you never even committed.
It fills you with fear,
Fears that don't even exist.

It makes you feel underrated,
For the things you excel at,
And makes you feel too much,
For simply giving what you can.

It judges you,
Stares at you,
Awaiting with its mouth agape
And arms wide open–
But not to create a heaven,
But to build a living hell.

It frightens me,
How love gets reciprocated with lust,
How truth is met with a lie,
And kindness is responded with hurt.
Sometimes,
The world just scares me.

Me To My Traumatized Inner Child
Only if I could ghost you,
For a moment,
To appease you and whisper,
"Hey, everything is going to be okay".

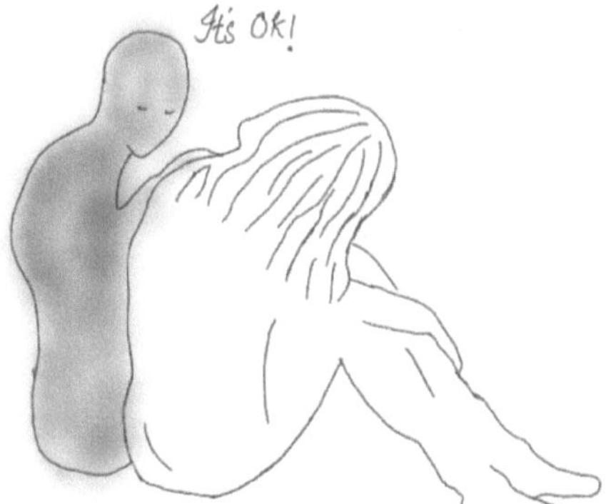

REALISATIONS TO SELF

A brief synopsis
The "Mental" Math We Weren't Taught In Schools:

Avoiding your emotions = Multiplying your emotions.
Not learning from your experiences = Merely accumulating and galloping your traumas.
Not feeling the pain = Trauma has already taken hold.
Not accepting your mistakes = Resisting your healing.
Collecting red flags = Cutting out space for the green ones.
The only lessons you truly learn = The ones you choose to implement.
Other people's reaction = Their perception of who you are.
Your reaction to others reaction = A projection of your perception of self.
Harboring negative emotions = Storing trauma within your body.
Harboring unresolved trauma in your body = Manifesting physical pain and unease.
Tolerating toxicity = Imbibing toxicity.
Getting triggered without awareness = Reacting mindlessly.
Getting triggered and choosing awareness = Responding mindfully.
Not being easily triggered = Standing on the threshold of wisdom.

Plants,
Maintenance demands care,
Undivided timely attention,
And nurturing.
Anything lacking would result in a severe dropping.
A withering that's hard to reverse.
The same goes for nourishing a human heart.

I've been sitting with my heart lately…

Diseased Body
You believe it's your body that aches,
But it's your subconscious expressing itself.
By ignoring, dumping, and suppressing your emotions there,
You turned a blind eye to their quiet pleas.

Now, they shout back,
Expressing themselves through your body.
Listen closely–
Your conscience whispers,
And your body mediates this conversation.

Your body: the gateway through which your mind expresses itself.

Your body speaks.
It communicates.
So just pay heed.

It reveals when it feels safe,
When it's comfortable with someone's energy,
And when it feels threatened by another's presence.
It conveys the difference between a glare and a stare,
Rejecting an unhealthy touch,
And cherishing a healthy one.
It can tell when lust surrounds it,
And when love has truly captivated it.

Your body listens,
It feels,
And it communicates.

Pay attention.
Lend an ear.

When you feel the urge to leave a toxic place–
A place that has left you with nothing but hurt,
Shame, and resentment–
Dark chains will try to hold you back.
Yet, amidst the shadows,
There may be one bleak light, one good thing,
Waiting agape tirelessly,
Ready for you to grasp it.

I urge you: follow that light.
Hold onto that one good omen.
It will guide you to a thousand more.

A gentle reminder–
Find your tiny wooden plank, even in deep waters.

It's your lifeline, your way back to shore–
Safe and whole again.

Through The Depths

Initially,
Pain tastes like slow poison,
That's being injected into your veins,
Dripping down, numbing your body,
And gradually pulling you into oblivion.

You might think
It will consume you entirely.
It feels endless, relentless–
A shadow that devours from within.

But then comes the day,
The day you believe you have had too much.
Instead of crumbling under fear and weakness,
You rise– fearless, strong and bold.
Because only by diving deep,
Gasping through the darkness,
You learn to surface again.

Healed.
Resilient.
Whole.

Because only after going through it you grow.

You see?
We humans–
We grow, we learn,
Through our pain,
Through our sadness.

Yet somehow,
We've confined happiness
To fleeting celebrations,
Moments of festivity,
While forgetting its deeper roots.

True joy isn't a spark—it's a quiet resilience,
Not just laughter, but lessons,
Woven through the shadows we've endured.

Distance yourself from people,
And you'll see them in a different light.
A shift in perspective–
One you never noticed when standing too close.

Distance reveals how close they truly are to you.
Distance reveals how near you truly are to them.
It uncovers the substrate that glued you together,
The hidden foundation,
Or the cracks you overlooked.

With distance,
Your eyes find a new window,
Viewing the familiar in unfamiliar ways.
Your mind gains fresh insight,
And the truth gently unfolds.

The world is brimming with mixed energies.
Crying over the chaos won't help.
It's on you to decide,
Which energy you align with,
What you embrace,
And what you discard.

It's the note you touch,
That decides the music you play.

If you measure your righteousness and affability
Through the lens of others,
Then you are mistakenly doomed.

If you wish to dwell in peace,
With your perception of self,
Learn the art of letting go,
By resisting the pull to take everything personally.

What others do,
What they say or how they behave,
Speaks volumes of their inner battles,
And whispers little about your essence.

Forgive them,
Pray for their healing,
And guard your peace with gentle resilience.

Our entire lives,
We strive to be
"Somebody," "Someday".

And yet,
Amid this endless pursuit,
We somehow fail
To be ourselves.

An irony etched
On the fabric of human existence.

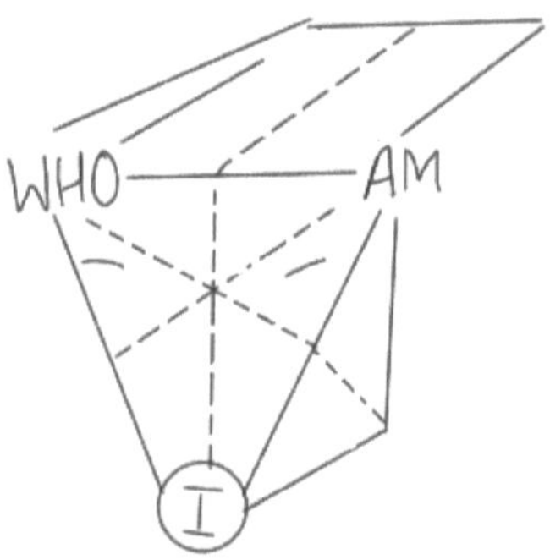

The Lingering Shadow

I knew I was flawed.
Harboring my share of dark thoughts.
So, to cleanse them
I choose to confront the depths within–
Via exploring my shadow side.

The dark,
Foggy,
Translucent specter.

The shadow,
Lingering at the edges of my being,
Waiting.
Not to be exiled,
But to be seen.
Seeking reverence for its existence.

Take The Wheel
For this instance,
Let's abandon the blame game,
The comforting delusion
Of always being the victim,
The one played with,
The indecisive one in the room.

Pause.
Take responsibility–
For "letting it happen to you",
For the choices that led you astray,
For the ignorance you subjected yourself to,
The negativity you endured,
The traumas you accepted as your own.

Change the script.
This time, confront yourself.

Always blaming others, blaming fate–
It leaves you powerless,
A bystander in your own life.

Take charge.
Grip the wheel with purpose,
And lead it through the storms,
Like a victorious warrior.

Having rigid perceptions
Is narrowing your mind's horizons.
But fathom this:
Your consciousness knows no bounds,
No constrictions.

So, why build walls
That shut you away from the skies?
Instead, build ladders,
That gets you there.

Unleash

Realizing this truth:
You have nothing to lose,
For you never truly owned
Anyone or anything.

This realization
It doesn't break you,
It makes you bold,
It sets you free.

For once,
Let go of your hyper–independent era.
It's ok to be taken care of by someone.

It's ok if you can't show up for yourself today–
This time, let somebody else do it for you.
It's ok to be showered with love,
To allow yourself to trust its warmth.

It's ok to peep beyond the curtains you draw,
To look outside and feel safe,
For what awaits on the other side of the window
Might be the solace you've long deserved.

Love: Return On Infatuation
We don't love,
Because "we are love".
We love,
Because "we get something out of it".

We want to be with someone
Because we are getting our motives justified,
And our desires met.
The idea of love is not enough
To sustain us in it.

We don't love
Because "we want to love them",
We don't love
Because we wish for their happiness.
We don't yearn to be the givers,
If our needs of receiving are unmet.

Our love is not an organically perpetuating emotion,
Nor a state of being,
But a reaction to what we receive,
When we give.

And that's the saddest part
Of how we perceive love–
A weak conditional pursuit
Driven by what we gain, when we give.

Love!
My dear,
Shouldn't be a hustle.

BEING LOVE

The most tiresome fight one can indulge in is a battle against oneself– a struggle between you and your self–deployed negative thoughts.
Between you and a voice blaring inside your head– commanding you to stop and turn motionless.
Your inner spark of light struggles to stay alive against the overwhelming splashes of darkness your subconscious attempts to impose.
It's a battle of hopes versus fears,
A struggle where one-foot pushes forward,
While the other pulls back.
A fight between uncharted risks and embraced opportunities.

However, modifying my initial statement,
The most courageous battle is the one fought with no one else but yourself.
A battle where your positive self, defeats doubt,
Where your quiet strength overpowers the noise urging you to stop.
A battle where a single spark grows into a blazing fire and wades away the darkness.
And where your genuine hopes shine brighter than your false fears.
Even with wounds and setbacks,
Your feet move forward, leaving behind the footprints for generations to follow.
A battle worth every win!

Peaceful Bloom

Your happiness
Should not be a reaction to what's around you.
Your happiness
Should be an expression of the peace within.

For those who wish to change a bad habit they have or a painful past,
I know you feel stagnant.
I know you are waiting for someone to hold your hand and guide you through.
I know you are searching for the right moment, waiting for the hard times to pass.
I know your eyes have been longing for light, to sway the darkness.
I know you believe that "this pain" has shaped your thoughts and reflects in who you are.

Let me tell you something –
Yes, someone is waiting for you to hold your hand and lead you to the light.
That person is the voice deep within you, urging you to take that first baby step.
Yes, **that person is you.**
Yes, the right moment you are waiting for exists, and that moment is **now**– the very moment you decide to embrace self–improvement and make a change.
No matter how hard the journey, there is always room to grow and time to evolve.
And there is no better beginning than to begin now.

When the context of questioning shifts from outward to inward,
A cycle of reflection and rumination follows.

Ruminating on fears, flaws, and weaknesses,
Overthinking them endlessly,
Can lead you into a spiral of depression and anxiety.

On the flip side,
Reflecting upon your inner self,
Where the driving force is not fear,
But an inner calling– an urge to know yourself and grow,
Brings you closer to discovering your true potential.

After a series of self–loathing and struggle,
Reflection will lead you to find peace within yourself.

Sometimes,
You don’t fully grasp
How far you’ve come,
Until you meet people
Still juggling with the lies,
Lies they live as their reality.

Sometimes,
You don’t fully grasp
How far you need to travel,
Until you encounter those
Who have mastered
The art of living the truth.

Be your own hero,
Before you wander off to find one.
Accept yourself with all your flaws,
Before waiting for someone to accept them.

Amend your mistakes,
Before wishing to be fixed by others.
Heal yourself from your traumas,
Before sobbing over someone and wishing them to mend your wounds.

Love yourself,
Before yearning for love from anyone else.

You can be both **strong** and **sensitive.**
You don't have to act cold to protect yourself.
Cold is contagious,
While being **sensitively strong** is courageous.

It's facile to lose yourself,
Far easier than it sounds,
Far simpler than you might conceive–
To drop your bundle of intrinsic assets,
To surrender,
Just because it's effortless,
And momentarily comforting.

There's a world that works tirelessly,
To see you unravel,
To pull you under.

And then there's another world,
One that holds you steady,
One that sends you good omens of hope,
Urging you to remain raw,
To stay resolute.

Both the worlds operate within you,
Both worlds are for you to choose from.

Home In The Hearts We Keep

Keep them close–
The ones who silently pray for your happiness,
The ones working in the background
To craft your million–dollar laughter and billion–dollar smile.

The one's not faking trust.
Who leave no stone unturned
To bring back the lost smile on your sad face.
The one's who feel like home–
A home with distinctively colored walls,
Each embracing the presence of the other.

A home, that nurtures your growth,
That witnesses your becoming.
A place to retreat, to pause–
Where, after taking a day off from your sufferings,
You go to feel loved and safe.

A virtual tight hug to the ones.

Go shower yourself with special pregnancy treatment.
Intend your soul, like a baby being nurtured inside you.
Your little creation.
The one who would eat what you eat,
Who would drink what you drink,
Who would absorb what you think,
And who would imprint the memory,
Of what you experience.
Who will reflect the love you give,
The care you offer.
Who will flourish with the energy you nurture it.

Spoiling myself with self–love lately.

Life's unfair serving,
Don't grant you an excuse to serve others sinfully,
Nor does it render you with an excuse to lead astray.

The clouds will clear,
The smoke will disperse,
Unclogging the pores,
Making space for abundant blessings to flow in.

The Listener Beyond Silence
Believe in the power of truth,
Believe in his care and protection.
Worry not about the amount of sadness he places in your lap–
For the lap is designed to hold only what he gives.

Quantify not the amount of happiness you wish to receive,
For the lap holds what is pre–destined,
More goodness than you could ever imagine.
So, empty the lap of your worries,
And create space for the blessings
You never expected, never asked for.

He is listening,
Even when you don't speak.
He is listening
To your sobbing,
To your laughter.

He is witnessing you–
With you,
For you,
Within you.

Healing (accepting the light that you are)

The Serenity Of Letting Go

There is peace,
In not recklessly piercing your thoughts,
In not losing arrows blindly into the air.

There is peace,
In letting life transcend placidly,
Without burdening it with the load of expectations.

There is peace,
In surrendering the wheel of situations
You were never meant to steer.

There is peace,
In letting go–
Letting go of the expectations of unforeseen,
Letting go of the fear of the undesired,
Allowing life to unfold,
As it was always destined to.

There is peace,
In surrendering to love.
In surrendering to light.

There is peace,
In taking a leap of faith,
And walking the tides.

Harmony In The Tempest

"~~Finding~~ Being peace, within chaos",
Has always been, and will forever remain,
The greatest blessing a human endows
During his lifetime on this earth.

Speak to those boulders
About your God,
And watch them pulverize,
See them erode,
As they pave the way for you to walk through.

I open my eyes,
And I go sightless.
I close my eyes,
And I begin to see.
When I breathe consciously,
The inner dots connect–
And I am set free.

The Vision

It is in the moment of nothingness within your mind,
That you become everything.
The 'you' in you–
Dissolves.

When you turn inward,
You hold the magic wand
To transform everything outward.

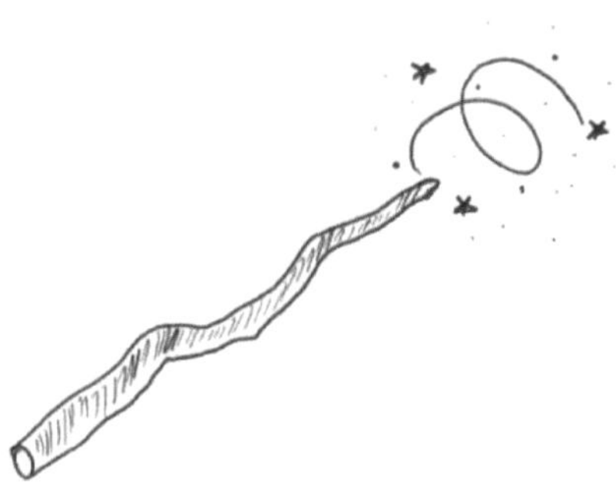

Regardless of how bleak the light seems,
Pray for–
Vision to see,
Courage to accept,
Strength to walk.

The path.

Everything she touched,
Turned mystical.

She was undergoing ecdysis,
Transforming into a walking euphoria.

Every catastrophe is an opportunity.
Fiercer the storm,
The greater the opportunity it presents,
To sanctify your inner being.

To the one,
Who chose self–negligence and self–flagellation,
To make someone feel okay,
Please!
Let go of the need to be agreeable.
Drop the imposition of unconscious decisions
That lead you into trouble.

Instead, inculcate consciousness into practice.
Accept your imperfections,
And allow others to see you as imperfect.
You are not here to strive for perfection.

Accept your wholeness,
Which comes with a potion of imperfection.
And in this imperfection–
In being truly you,
Lies your victories,
Your defeats,
Your capabilities,
And your shortcomings.

All of it shapes you,
Makes you whole,
Complete,
And truly human.

Love,
Is not possession.
It's liberation.

What a home should feel like:
Safe.
Comfortable.
Affable.

Where do you go to find your home?
You go to yourself.

You, thyself, should be your home.
Comfortable in your own skin.
Safe with your own thoughts.
And affable in your actions directed inward.

Only then will you find a companion
To share your home with.
Only then will you find a companion,
Whom you designate as your home–
With whom you are truly yourself.
With whom it feels safe.
With whom you feel loved and devoted.

Anything less
Is not your home.

I am coming Home.

ARE YOU?

www.ingramcontent.com/pod-product-compliance
Ingram Content Group UK Ltd.
Pitfield, Milton Keynes, MK11 3LW, UK
UKHW041348190726
13845UKWH00026B/482

9 789334 353365